Scary Stories for Kids Age 9-12

Spooky, Short Ghost Tales and
Mysterious Adventures for Campfires,
Sleepovers, and Halloween Fun

Nicole Goodman

Contents

Chapter 1

All eyes on Kevin

It was Kevin's tenth birthday, and for the first time ever, he had the entire house to himself. His parents, both busy doctors, were out of town for a conference. They had wished him a happy birthday that morning over a video call and mentioned a surprise gift for him, which would arrive later in the evening. But they hadn't said what it was.

Excited, Kevin invited all his friends over for a birthday party. By the time dusk arrived, the house was filled with music and laughter. The party was in full swing, and Kevin was having the time of his life. As more of his school friends started to arrive, the birthday boy noticed that the snack bowls were running low. He made his way to the kitchen, which was at the end of a narrow hallway, to refill them.

As he stepped into the kitchen and started filling the plates with snacks, a faint knock interrupted his action. Kevin paused, listening intently. The knock came again, louder this time. He turned his head towards the back door, where the sound was coming from. He stepped closer to the door, and with a flick turned on the backyard lights.

He slowly peeked through the keyhole and what he saw made his heart skip a beat. Standing right outside, almost sticking itself to the doorframe, was a BIRTHDAY CLOWN. It was the kind of clown you'd see at a circus—bright red hair, white face paint, a big red nose, and an exaggerated smile. It was holding a single red balloon, and attached to its suit was a big white card that read, "For Kevin."

The clown was for him? Kevin thought, getting amused but not scared. He wasn't afraid of clowns. Rather, he found them entertaining.

However, there was something about this one that made him wonder whether to welcome him or not. Just then, his friend Boris wandered into the kitchen.

"What are you looking at?" Boris asked.

"There's a birthday clown outside that has my name written on its suit. My parents had mentioned a surprise earlier but I had no idea this was it." Kevin told Boris.

Boris spotted the clown through the keyhole and nudged Kevin. "That is one scary clown. Your parents really know how to surprise someone!" Boris chuckled, and soon the boys welcomed the clown inside the house.

"I'm Kevin. You must be the surprise my parents sent, right?" Kevin asked with curiosity.

No answer. The clown just stood beside the doorframe and stared at Kevin with its big, brown eyes and an exaggerated smile.

"Did you bring any gifts? Or perhaps you'll show some tricks." Boris asked with a chuckle as he stepped closer, but his laughter quickly faded when he noticed that the clown wasn't even looking at him. His eyes were only fixed on Kevin.

Again, there was no reply from the clown. Somehow that irritated Kevin so he ignored its presence and asked Boris to follow him back to the party.

While at the party Kevin grabbed his phone and quickly texted his dad, "Received your surprise."

The party continued, and Kevin tried to ignore the unsettling feeling that someone was watching him. And he was right! Every now and then he'd glance down the hallway towards the kitchen, and each time, he saw the clown standing in the same spot, staring at him with a painted, unwavering smile.

"Doesn't it feel like the clown is always watching you?" Boris asked later, feeling uneasy. "I mean, it's kind of creepy, right?"

Kevin forced a laugh and shook his head. "It's just a clown, Boris. No big deal." But even as he said it, he couldn't deny that his courage was starting to vanish.

Kevin's phone buzzed, signaling that it was nearly dead. He excused himself from the party and headed upstairs to his room to charge it.

The music and laughter from the living room started to fade as he climbed the stairs.

His room was dark when he entered, the only light coming from the street lamp outside casting a faint glow through the curtains. Kevin walked to his bedside, plugged his phone into the charger, and turned to leave... when his heart stopped.

"Huhh," he gasped in horror.

Standing in the doorway was the clown. Its smile was as wide and eerie as ever, and its eyes locked onto Kevin's with an intensity that made him freeze.

"What are you doing here?" Kevin stammered, his voice barely above a whisper.

The clown didn't respond.

"Do you need something?" Kevin asked, and this time the clown slowly and silently reached into its pocket and pulled out a letter, handing it to Kevin with a slow, deliberate motion. Kevin hesitated, his fingers trembling as he took the letter. The clown watched him the entire time, its eyes never leaving his.

He was so startled by the clown's sudden presence in his room that Kevin didn't even bother to open the piece of paper and read its contents. Instead, he asked the clown to follow him downstairs where the party was going on.

The clown nodded ever so slightly and followed Kevin down the stairs, almost like his shadow. Once back in the kitchen, the clown returned to its original spot, standing silently by the door, still holding that red balloon.

The night dragged on, and eventually, the party came to an end. Kevin's friends started saying their goodbyes and soon everyone left, leaving the house eerily quiet. Kevin was dog-tired but he had one final thing to do before he called it a day; to make the creepy clown leave.

Kevin marched into the kitchen with a sudden found braveness, expecting to see the clown still standing by the door. But it was gone. The backdoor was slightly ajar, and the balloon was nowhere to be seen.

*That's weird...*Kevin thought. However, he was relieved that the clown had finally left.

He headed upstairs to his room and plopped down on his bed when suddenly...

BRRRINGGG!!!

BRRRINGGG!!!

His phone rang. It was Dad calling.

"Hey, son! How was the party?" Kevin's dad inquired.

"Everything was great, dad, except for the surprise birthday clown. It was sooo weird," Kevin said, and had an unpleasant feeling while mentioning the clown.

His dad paused on the other end of the line. "What clown? We didn't hire any birthday clown, Kevin. Your surprise is a new bicycle. It was supposed to arrive today but now they are saying it will be delivered tomorrow."

Kevin froze. His face turned pale.

His dad must have sensed something was wrong as he became alarmed. "Kevin, listen to me carefully. Did you let any strangers into the house?"

Kevin's mind raced and his body shook. However, he knew how important this conference was so he didn't want to scare his parents and make them worry. So, he lied, "No, I didn't let anyone in. I'm fine, dad. I was just checking. Don't worry."

After ending the call, Kevin was frightened. He quickly opened his phone and pulled up the security camera feed. His parents had installed security cameras a few years ago and they finally came in handy.

His hands trembled as he played the footage from the party and watched in growing horror as the camera showed the clown standing at the back door. Kevin realized how big of a mistake he had made by allowing a stranger inside the house and was relieved that the clown had left earlier.

Kevin then remembered how the clown had handed him some paper and he hurriedly picked it up and read what looked like a disturbing message; **I'm Always Watching You!**

If he wasn't afraid of clowns before, now he absolutely was. Panicking, Kevin tried to check the rest of the CCTV footage when something horrific caught his eye.

The video showed the clown suddenly moving while Kevin was saying goodbye to his friends in the living room. However, the clown didn't leave through the backdoor as Kevin had thought.

Instead, when nobody was watching, it walked up the stairs, its movements slow and steady.

Kevin watched the video, paralyzed, as the clown entered his room and creepily slid under the bed.

Kevin felt trapped in his own house, shaking, and terrified. The house was eerily quiet and he ever so slowly looked down, his palm sweating and heart pounding.

And then he saw it.

Peeking from underneath his bed was the clown, its painted white face twisted into a grin, its eyes shining with excitement, staring right at him.

Just like he promised. He was always watching Kevin.

The house wasn't quiet anymore...Kevin's spine-chilling scream echoed through the empty abode. After that he wasn't seen anymore, disappearing into thin air.... *For ever and ever....*

YOUR FREE GIFT AWAITS!

Thank you for choosing to explore our spooky tales! As a special "thank you" for your purchase, we're excited to offer you a copy of our book **"Knock Knock Jokes for Kids"**—absolutely FREE! (Regularly priced at $9.99 on Amazon). Inside, you'll discover over **500 hilarious jokes** that promise hours of laughter and fun for the whole family. But that's not all! You'll also gain exclusive access to opportunities for more FREE books from us in the future.

To claim your free gift, simply visit: bit.ly/43WKetK

Or scan the QR code below with your camera.

Enjoy, and thank you for being a valued reader!

Chapter 2

Clap in the Dark

The summer night was breezy and perfect for a camping trip. The stars twinkled above, and the cold air was ideal for a bonfire. On top of a mountain gathered around the bonfire was a family of three enjoying the camp night.

The place was surrounded by dense woods and tall trees, the type that gave the surrounding area a creepy vibe. The father poked at the fire while his wife sat nearby, their young son nestled close to her.

"Time for a scary story." The father smirked, looking at his son, who wasn't a big fan of scary stories.

"Stop scaring him. Let's just sit and enjoy the beauty," the mother interfered, hugging her son tight.

The boy, no older than nine, smiled at his mother. Suddenly, a rustling sound came from the forest, startling him. The boy's heart skipped a beat, and he clutched his mother's hand tightly.

"Mom, what was that?" he whispered with wide eyes.

His mother squeezed his hand reassuringly. "It's probably just the wind, sweetheart. Don't worry."

"Let me check." The father stood up with a stick in his hand and walked over to the trees.

The wife called out to her husband in distress, "Wait. Maybe it's best if we all just stay together. What if there's....?"

"There's nothing to be afraid of. What can harm us anymore?" the father interrupted with a chuckle.

His wife fell silent, her expression unhappy, while their son looked back and forth between his parents with a confused look. The father shook his head and headed toward the dark forest. The crunching of leaves under his feet scared whoever was hiding in the forest as they emerged from behind a tree.

A girl, around the age of twelve, stepped forward.

She looked frightened and was shivering in her torn and dirty clothes. Her long hair covered most of her pale face. The father's eyes softened— *What was such a young girl doing at this time all alone?*

"Are you lost?" he asked gently. "Where are your parents?"

The girl didn't answer. She simply shook her head and pointed to her throat, indicating that she was mute.

"Can you understand me?" the father asked.

The girl nodded.

"Follow me then," he said. "My family's right over here. We'll help you find your way back."

He led the girl back to the campfire, where his wife and son watched with wide eyes. "She's lost," the father explained. "And she can't talk. We'll let her stay with us tonight, and in the morning, we'll help her find her parents."

The wife smiled kindly at the girl and spoke, "You must be so scared, poor thing. But you're safe with us."

The girl returned her smile when the father came up with an idea. "How about this? One clap for yes, two claps for no. That way, we can understand you better. Is that okay?"

Clap.... The girl clapped once.

"Good," the wife said. "Let's get some rest. We'll start looking for your family first thing in the morning. You came with your parents for camping, right?"

One clap.

The family set up a small tent for the girl and settled into their own tent nearby. The fire burned low, and soon the night was quiet again.

Everyone retired to their tents, leaving the place quiet and peaceful except for the occasional hooting of owls.

A few hours passed by, and the night deepened. It was past three in the night and inside her tent, the girl's eyes snapped open. Carefully she sat up, not wanting to make any noise, and reached into her pocket.

She had a wicked smile on her face as she pulled out a wad of cash.

"They were so easy to fool," she whispered. "Too trusting, just like all the others."

The girl could speak.

She and her father had been pulling this scam for years, preying on innocent campers. The father would rob couples while the girl was tasked with tricking families.

While the family had been busy earlier, she had already slipped the bundle of cash into her pockets without them noticing. Now, all she had to do was sneak out, meet up with her father, and disappear into the night.

Quietly, she stepped out of the tent, but something felt off.

The air was chilly, and the once warm and lively campsite looked different. The tents appeared old and worn, as if they had been abandoned for years. The fire was completely out, leaving the place dark and gloomy.

"What's going on?" the girl whispered, a shiver running down her spine.

She tip-toed towards the other tent where the family was asleep and peeked inside. Her eyes widened as there was no sign of anyone inside and only a foul smell was left behind.

The tent had holes everywhere and the sleeping bags had mold and dirt as if no one had slept there for years.

This isn't possible. I saw them getting inside. The girl thought and pulled out the money she had stolen earlier to make herself believe she wasn't dreaming.

However, she was startled to find that the stack was old and crumpled as if it had been in her pocket for decades.

Fear started to creep in and she felt cold.

Her eyes then fell on a newspaper that lay near the bonfire. She picked it up and saw the newspaper was dated a year ago. She turned the pages when an image scared her stiff.

Family of Three Dies During A Camping Trip – The article's headline read. The family was engulfed by the campfire that had burned out of control while they were asleep.

At the end of the article was a picture of the family. Her hands trembled as she looked at the picture and she threw the paper away.

Panic set in as the picture was of the same people who had given her shelter earlier.

"This isn't possible. They were here. I saw them," she whispered frantically.

In a flash of terror, the girl realized; she wasn't the one fooling them – they let her.

"Then what I saw... they were ghosts?"

As soon as she finished her sentence, she heard it—a sound that made her blood run cold.

Clap Clap.... Clap Clap.... Clap Clap.

The same claps she used to fool the family.

The girl's scream was engulfed by the deadly night and soon the forest returned to its peaceful silence.

Sometimes, on a quiet night... the family returns to the campsite to wait for their next victim.

Chapter 3

The Scary Scarecrow

Mark's summer vacation was coming to an end soon and up until now, it wasn't eventful. His parents were too busy to take him on a trip, so when Uncle Ben asked Mark to look after his countryside house while he was gone for a few days, he was ecstatic.

The house wasn't big, but it was quite far from the city and Mark liked the idea of enjoying the peaceful country life.

He could hardly keep himself from jumping for joy, for this was his first time living alone in a house like this. Mark noticed that crop fields surrounded the house on three sides except the main entrance, and the nearest house was about fifteen to twenty minutes away by foot – perfect for an introvert like him.

"I guess Uncle Ben likes to be all alone," Mark expressed, noticing the quiet surroundings.

However, he wasn't alone.

From the bedroom window, Mark saw the fields stretched out far and wide, but there was a figure that caught his eye—a scarecrow.

Standing tall on the left side, it faced the house, doing its job well – watching the crop field.

But something about the scarecrow made Mark feel uneasy.

More specifically, its eyes and how real they looked.

It is supposed to scare off birds, not me. Mark thought and chuckled.

Later that night, Mark found himself having trouble sleeping. The place was quiet. Almost too quiet. He tossed and turned for a few minutes, finally starting to doze off, but then a loud thud woke him up. Mark's eyes snapped open, and he quickly sat up in bed, breathing heavily. The clock read almost 2 AM.

The place fell silent and Mark was about to fall asleep when....

Thump! There was the sound again, now louder and stronger, like something was moving right outside the house.

Mark got up, crept to the window, and peeked out with curiosity and what he saw made him sigh in relief and put a hand over his pounding heart.

There was a small dog in the yard, sniffing around. Mark wondered why he hadn't noticed the dog earlier but wasn't bothered because he was fond of animals.

He tapped on the window happily, hoping to catch the dog's attention, making the animal look up. And what he saw made his blood run cold....

The dog had no eyes, just empty, dark sockets staring right at him.

Mark stumbled back from the window, his lips trembling and hands shaking.

"What the hell was that?" Mark muttered to himself, completely shocked and clueless.

He looked outside the window again and the dog was nowhere to be found. The scarecrow was standing there, facing the house, like always.

Either way, Mark was very disturbed by the scarecrow and the dog, which he believed was a figment of his imagination. So, he shut the curtains and walked away from the window, leaving the scarecrow to stare on.

His sleep was now long gone so Mark went downstairs to drink some water. The house creaked in the dark with each step Mark took and by the time he reached the kitchen, Mark wanted to leave the place as soon as possible.

The next morning, Mark stood under the bedroom window and watched the place where he had seen the dog digging some dirt and to his surprise, there were no claw marks! Mark was confused but decided to forget about it, and went about his day.

As night approached, Mark was ready for bed again. He locked the windows, drew the curtains, and was determined to get a good night's sleep. In the dead of night, Mark was sleeping soundly and the house was quiet when....

A howling in the distance broke the peace.

Mark woke up. Startled and scared, he slowly made his way towards the window. And what he saw didn't help him at all. Outside the window, the scarecrow was looking at him as usual.

However, he started to get terrified. His sleep was long gone so he ran downstairs to get some water to calm his nerves.

In haste he filled up a glass and gulped down the water, his eyes squeezed shut. Once he was done and was ready to return to his room his gaze drifted to the window that looked out over the field.

Mark froze.

The scarecrow was now standing in front of the kitchen window, staring at him with those real-looking eyes.

Overcome by fear, Mark could not move; his body grew numb. It was supposed to be on the other side of the house, only visible from the bedroom window. Did someone change its place?

Suddenly, as if a spell was broken, Mark could finally move his body. He hurried upstairs, locking the door. He had no more courage left to look out the window so he got into bed.

That night, Mark barely got any sleep.

And shockingly, the next morning, the scarecrow outside the kitchen window was gone - at least, the one he imagined he had seen there last night. The only scarecrow he could see was the one in the field.

Mark felt a small sense of relief. Maybe it was all just a bad dream. The dog, the other scarecrow... Mark convinced himself that his imagination was running wild.... He was running almost crazy.

However, deep down he knew that something was wrong. *Very wrong*.

And just like that sleep didn't come easily that night. Weirdly there was no dog howling in the distance or any faint rustling in the yard. But an unknown fear kept Mark on edge as he spent the whole night sitting on his bed and staring out the window.

The next morning, Mark was overjoyed, ready to leave the creepy place. His uncle was returning that day, so Mark packed his things and locked the house.

The eyes glowing under the sunlight made the boy wonder if the scarecrow's sole purpose was to watch the house instead of the field.

A chill ran down Mark's spine as he turned away and walked quickly to the bus stop.

On the bus ride home, Mark's phone rang. It was his Uncle Ben.

Mark was relieved and answered it quickly. Uncle Ben thanked him for taking care of the house *all alone*.

"I wasn't all alone if you count the scarecrow watching the house with its almost real-looking eyes." Mark laughed, although he was still somewhat nervous.

There was a long pause on the other end. Mark started feeling uneasy. He had read scary books and most of the time this was the part where the person would say 'What Scarecrow?' or 'There wasn't any Scarecrow.'

However, what his uncle said next made Mark break into a cold sweat.

"The scarecrow has no eyes, Mark. It never did. There was a dog who used to guard it.... He was blind. Years ago, when the dog died the people around there decided to leave the scarecrow as it is... with no eyes. They did it as a sign of respect." Uncle Ben's voice was low and serious.

The call ended and Mark felt his stomach drop. He stared out the window, his mind racing, trying to make sense of what his uncle had just said.

He never got an answer, but he knew those things he saw... they weren't his imagination.

Mark never spoke of the incident again, and neither did he tell his parents.

And months later when he heard that his uncle had sold the house, Mark couldn't shake the feeling that something was still out there, in the fields.... watching... waiting.

Chapter 4

The Lost Toy

I t was Noah and his family's last day camping. The setting sun cast long shadows across the campsite as the family packed their things. Noah was busy stuffing his backpack when he noticed something missing. His best buddy, Teddy—a scruffy, well-loved teddy bear that had been with him since eternity.

"Mom! Dad! I cannot find Teddy!" Noah declared, looking around frantically.

"Maybe you left him near the tent?" Ava, his sister, suggested, but he wasn't buying it.

Teddy was gone and Noah's heart sank as he realized it. The night was approaching and his parents were eager to hit the road before nightfall. So, Noah's mom promised to buy him a new one when they reached home.

"No one can replace Teddy," Noah said, heartbroken. To him, Teddy wasn't just a toy.

"We promise we will buy you the same teddy bear. Now hop inside." Noah's dad tried to cheer him up and as the sky darkened, the family climbed into the car.

The car left the campsite and the sky turned a shade darker as they drove towards their destination. Noah could see thunder rumbling in the distance, just above their camping site, and soon rain pitter-pattered on the car roof.

They all were relieved to get out of the forest just in time... *except for someone*.

Back in the forest, as the storm intensified, something strange happened.

In the bushes, Teddy laid motionless where Noah had dropped him unknowingly when he and his father were exploring the thick woods. The toy lay still, soaked by the rain.

Suddenly, bats started circling the sky, screeching. The wind howled and the forest seemed to be on the lookout. In the middle of the chaos, a flash of lightning lit up the sky, and in that brief second, Teddy's eyes glowed.

A dull, eerie light.

An hour later, the family reached home and Noah went straight to his room. They were all tired from the journey and were ready to go to bed.

Upon entering his room, Noah threw himself onto his bed, hugging his pillow tight. He missed Teddy.

That night, the house was eerily quiet as the family slept. The storm had followed them home, and rain tapped against the windows, creating a gloomy atmosphere around the house.

Noah, deep in his slumber, suddenly woke up to a soft thud. He blinked in the darkness, wondering what it was.

He sat up slowly, and that's when he felt it—something warm and familiar hugging him under the blanket. He looked down and gasped in surprise.

"Teddy?" he whispered in disbelief.

Snuggling against him was his stuffed bear as if it had never been lost. Noah hugged Teddy tightly, a smile spreading across his face.

"How did you get here?" Noah asked no one in particular but then realized maybe it was his parents or his sister who had found Teddy in one of the bags and slipped it under his arm while he slept.

Relieved, Noah promised he would never lose Teddy again and went back to sleep.

The next day Noah woke up early to get ready for school. As they sat at the breakfast table, Noah asked his mom, "Did you find Teddy last night?"

"No, honey," his mom replied. "Maybe your dad or Ava did."

Noah asked Ava, but she too denied it. "I guess Dad found it. Ask him once he comes back in the evening," Ava suggested, leaving Noah a little confused.

It was time for the bus and soon they were off to school.

Later that day, when the house was empty, Noah's mom decided to do some cleaning. She started with Noah's room and as she moved around, she stepped on something soft. Looking down, she saw it was Teddy.

The toy was lying on the floor, one arm slightly torn.

"Noah wouldn't be happy to see you like this. Let's stitch you up," she murmured and picked up the toy.

She stitched the arm up quickly and placed Teddy back on Noah's bed.

After a while, the house was quiet and the mother was in her room when she heard, "Mom! Mom!"

Noah was calling for her from downstairs.

She went still, frowning. *That's weird.... Noah should be at school.*

"Noah?" she called back, heading toward the staircase.

No answer.

Confused, she reached the top step when suddenly, she found herself losing her balance.

In a blink, she tumbled down the stairs, landing hard at the bottom with her arm twisted painfully.

While she slowly lost consciousness, her eyes saw some movement at the top of the staircase. The house wasn't as empty as she thought.

And then everything turned dark.

When the kids returned home, they found their dad tending to their mom who had to get a few stitches in her hand. They assured the kids that it was nothing serious and that they should avoid running down the stairs.

After the kids walked to their room, the mom confided in her husband.

"I heard Noah's voice," she whispered, her voice shaky. "But when I checked there was no one. And then suddenly... I felt like someone pushed me. I didn't slip... it was more like a shove from behind."

Her husband tried reassuring her, saying they were lucky nothing big happened. "When I saw you lying unconscious, I was shocked... .and," He paused. "And then beside you, I saw Noah's teddy bear. I thought maybe you slipped on it. Thank God, you are fine now."

Noah overheard the conversation. His heart began to race. He remembered the strange thud from the night before, the way Teddy had appeared so suddenly.

What if someone really pushed his mom? What if....

In the end, Noah wished nothing like this happened again.... *But how common is it for a wish to come true so soon?*

That night, the kids were studying together when Ava accidentally knocked over a glass of water. The water splashed on the floor, making a mess, but Ava realized that Teddy had gotten wet too, his fabric soaked most of the liquid.

"Oh no!" Ava said, quickly picking up Teddy. They had a drying rack near their pool area so she went there.

Leaving Teddy outside to dry, Ava turned around when she slipped and fell into the water.

She didn't know how to swim so she started screaming and thrashing, desperate to get out. Their parents heard her cries and raced outside. The dad dived into the pool just in time to save Ava.

Noah ran outside and saw his sister drenched in water and shivering. Her lips trembled as she spoke, "Push... some push..."

Ava was carried to her room as her body grew cold. Noah stood outside in the pool area, feeling suspicious. He slowly turned towards Teddy, who was on the chair, placed there by Ava. The toy was soaked, but something about its expression seemed... different.

Maybe it was his hunch.... but Noah was sure of one thing. Something about *his Teddy* was off.

That night, he couldn't sleep. Unlike most days, Noah wasn't hugging his bedtime pal. Teddy was kept in a corner of the room with the rest of his stuffed toys.

The next morning, Noah woke up with puffy and tired eyes. He hadn't slept a wink and luckily, his mom didn't force him to go to school.

Later that day Noah was playing quietly in his room, riding his toy bike around when suddenly he felt a bump. The bike ran over something.

Noah looked back and froze. It was Teddy.

His mind raced when he saw how the toy looked at him with its button eyes. Realizing his mistake, Noah quickly picked up Teddy and apologized to him countless times.

He was afraid of his best buddy. Very afraid.

As afternoon approached, Noah went with his mom to the doctor to get her stitches checked. The cuts were almost healed and the mother-son duo were happy about it.

On the way back, they stopped at a crosswalk. His mother was texting Noah's dad and the boy realized his shoelace had come loose. Noah bent down to tie his shoelaces, and suddenly... he felt a push.

In a flash, Noah stumbled forward, right into the middle of the road. His body froze when he saw a speeding car coming his way.

Everything went blank but then Noah felt someone yanking him back just in time. It was his mother.

People around them gathered while his mother hugged him tightly.

Shaking in fear, Noah realized this was no accident. It was the same push he knew his mom and sister felt.

And now, it tried to hurt him too.

Noah finally made up his mind. As soon as he got back home, he picked up Teddy with trembling hands and stuffed it into a box.

The toy wasn't his Teddy. It was something else. Something evil.

The next day, the family planned to go out for lunch and Noah brought the box with him, determined to get rid of Teddy once and for all.

"Are you sure about this?" Noah's mom asked.

Noah nodded saying, "I'm a big boy now. I don't need toys anymore." He kept the real reason for giving away his once-favorite buddy a deep, dark secret.

They drove down an empty alley and Noah asked his dad to stop the car.

He climbed out, carrying the box with him. He placed the box on the side of the road, giving it one last glance before returning to the car.

Teddy was left behind.

As they drove away, Noah felt a strange sense of relief.

But it wasn't over. Everyone was happy... except Teddy.

As the car disappeared into the distance, Teddy's eyes glowed with rage.

It was angry. How dare Noah abandon him! But it was going to be fine. Although Noah got rid of Teddy, he wouldn't leave Noah's side... ever.

Teddy was ready for his next move when a car approached him, forcing him to stay still.

The car stopped in front of the box Noah had left behind, and a door opened.

A little boy, much younger than Noah, stepped out, his eyes wide with excitement. He looked at Teddy and then back at his mom.

"Can I keep him, Mom? He looks so sad," the boy asked his mother.

His mother smiled and agreed, helping her son into the car with his new toy. As they drove away, Teddy sat quietly in the boy's arms, but if anyone had been watching, they might have noticed the wicked glow in its eyes.

For Teddy had found a new friend—a naïve, more innocent soul. And this time, he would make sure he wasn't abandoned again.

Chapter 5

Late Night Pizza

It was almost time to close the pizza shop and go home. Eddie was the last one to leave, and he was counting every second till the clock turned 10. Winter was around the corner and the streets were empty.

Eddie wiped down the counter, turned around the closed sign, and was finally done for the day. The place was finally peaceful after such a hectic day and the only sound was the soft hum of the fridge behind Eddie and the distant ticking of the wall clock.

He had just gathered his belongings and was reaching for the light switch when....

BRRRING! BRRRING!

The telephone rang.

Eddie jumped, startled. Who could be calling at this hour?

He felt weird, picking up the phone. "Thanks for calling Pizza Planet. How can I help you?"

On the other end was a woman's voice, "I'd like to order a pizza," her voice almost whispering.

"Sorry ma'am we're closed for the day," Eddie answered, checking the clock.

But the woman wouldn't take NO for an answer—or maybe she just didn't care. "I need a large pizza. Now." She insisted authoritatively, as if she were the boss.

Eddie sighed, glancing at the clock again. It was late. Too late. However, he remembered how the place had a rule – whoever takes a late-night order after the shop closes gets to keep the money to themselves. They didn't have to register the sale in the book.

Eddie could use some extra cash, so he reluctantly agreed. The woman gave her address and something about her voice made him uneasy.

She was persistent. But then all pizza lovers are. Eddie thought.

The delivery guy had already left so Eddie had to do the delivery himself. He packed the order and it was only after adding the address to the GPS on his phone that Eddie realized how secluded the area was.

Dejectedly, he grabbed his bike and set off into the dark as there wasn't any time to waste.

As he pedaled through the unfamiliar and empty streets, Eddie couldn't shake the feeling that taking the order was a mistake.

The streetlights were dim and the neighborhood was run down with no signs of any humans. If this was some other time, Eddie would have turned his bike and left. But he reminded himself how grumpy his boss was and if he found out Eddie would be fired on the spot.

Soon, he reached the building—an old, shabby apartment block that looked abandoned. Most of the windows were black, no lights on inside. He came to a stop and parked his bike.

The woman said she lived in apartment 31 and it looked like it was on the top floor of the building. Eddie walked past the entrance, whose walls were covered in dirt and mold. An old security guard was dozing off in a chair near the elevator and Eddie decided against waking up the elderly man.

The elevator dinged and Eddie walked into it. Inside it was too bright in contrast to the dark entrance of the building. The doors closed and slowly the elevator began to move up to the top floor.

After what felt like an eternity the movement stopped and when the doors finally slid open, Eddie's stomach dropped.

The hallway was dark. Too dark to see the numbers on the door.

Eddie took out his phone, turned on the flashlight, and started to walk down the narrow corridor. His steps were careful and calculated. The walls were peeling, the floor creaked under his shoes, and as he reached the far end of the hallway, he felt a sudden chill run down his body.

Turned out something about apartment 31 was odd.

There was something wrong with the door.

A large, red cross had been painted across it, bold and menacing. It gave Eddie the creeps. He wanted to run away but he couldn't. The woman had already paid online so Eddie wanted to get done with it.

His heart thudded in his chest as he knocked on the door. The sound echoed in the silence.

No answer.

KNOCK! KNOCK!

Eddie knocked again, louder and harder.

Still no response.

Maybe it's best to leave the pizza outside... Eddie thought, but the door creaked open. Barely.

The slow creaking noise alarmed him as he stepped back. The door was opened just enough for a pale, thin hand of a woman to slip out. Eddie could see the bones beneath the skin and it made him uneasy.

"Your pizza," Eddie stammered, thrusting the box forward, not wanting to see the person behind the door.

Eddie hurried back down the hallway, pressing the elevator button over and over. He was trembling when suddenly he realized something.

He didn't hear the door shut close. The sound never came which meant that whoever was waiting behind it was now watching him leave.

That terrified him to the core.

Eddie pressed the elevator button again, panic creeping into his veins. Finally, it arrived and for a second Eddie thought he heard footsteps behind him, but he refused to look back.

The elevator doors were closing and Eddie made the mistake of glancing back at the hallway.

It was empty.

He was sweating in such cold weather and the ride down was painfully slow.

When the doors opened, the guard was awake now, staring at Eddie with cold, narrowed eyes.

"What were you doing up there?" the guard asked, his voice rough and loud.

"I was delivering a pizza to apartment 31," Eddie replied, still trying to calm his racing heart.

The guard's expression darkened. He looked at Eddie weirdly.

"Stop lying. There's no apartment 31. 30 is the last one."

Eddie blinked; his face confused. "What do you mean? I just delivered a pizza there."

The guard took a step closer, his eyes boring into Eddie's. "There *used* to be Apartment 31. A couple died there. The wife poisoned her husband... over money, they say. She died shortly after. The building owner tore it down after people complained about getting strange vibes from there."

Eddie's throat went dry. That wasn't possible. He pulled out his phone to check the order, the money, anything to prove it had happened—but the payment was gone. The address wasn't there.

The guard's eyes then fell to the pizza shop logo on Eddie's shirt. "That's weird. That's the place she ordered from. Their pizza was the one she poisoned him with," he said before asking Eddie to leave.

Eddie staggered back, his head spinning. After that, he had no clue how he returned to the pizza shop....

And from that night on, Eddie never took a late-night order again.

Chapter 6

The Haunted Hotel

One late summer night, Liam was driving home from a trip. The road was empty except for a family car that almost passed by him an hour ago. Liam could easily reach his house in an hour or two but his eyes were heavy with sleep. A storm was also approaching, according to the man on the radio, and with no other choice Liam decided it would be safer to spend the night at a hotel.

A nearby hotel popped up in his search, just a ten-minute drive away.

"Better than to get caught in a storm," Liam muttered as a few drops of rain fell on the windscreen.

Upon reaching his destination, Liam found that the hotel was not very welcoming. However, the raging storm forced him to quickly grab his bag and lock the doors of his car before heading inside the building.

The place was small and isolated. If there were no lights in the hallway, anybody would think the hotel was abandoned. The entrance had a dimly lit bulb that flickered. Liam scared easily, which may have been why he had an uneasy feeling.

Thunder roared in the distance, but even the safety of four walls felt... creepy.

Like the lobby, the reception area had a single bulb flickering above a corner.

THUMP...THUMP.... Liam's footsteps echoed loudly as he approached the counter.

A man stood behind the desk. His face was mostly hidden under a dark, big cap, and his clothes had no name tag. Liam assumed he was the receptionist and asked, "Excuse me? I need a room for the night."

The man didn't greet Liam, nor did he raise his head.

This is weird.... Liam scrunched his eyebrows when the man slowly pulled out a dusty guestbook and started flipping through its pages. Liam could smell the dampness of the guestbook and it wasn't pleasant at all.

After what felt like an eternity, the receptionist stopped turning pages and pulled out a key, sliding it across the counter without saying a word.

Room 99. Liam glanced at the key and then back at the man. "Thanks...," he said awkwardly.

The man said nothing. *Again.*

In the end, Liam dragged his tired and sleepy self to Room 99. On his way, he couldn't help but notice something strange about the rooms on his floor – they were all locked. He couldn't shake the feeling that something was off. The hotel was so empty, and there was no sign of any other guests.

However, he was there for one night – Liam reassured himself. Nothing could go wrong in one night.

The room had a rundown door that was barely hanging on. Still, he was exhausted and wanted the night to be quickly over. The room was small, with a single bed and an old wooden table. It looked as if no one had stayed there in years.

The air was stale and chilly inside, and luckily the lights turned on when Liam flicked the switches. Despite the overall unsettling vibe from the hotel, the room wasn't too bad. Liam dropped his bag on the table, ready to hit the sack.

The clock showed 12:45 AM and he turned off the lights, hoping morning would arrive soon.

At exactly 1:30 AM, Liam woke up to a creaking noise.

He looked around, wondering what the sound was.

But there was nothing... until his eyes fell on the corner of the room.

Then he saw it—the bathroom door was ajar.

"That's weird. I remember closing it," Liam whispered in confusion.

Perhaps the door had loose screws or was not latched properly. Sighing, he walked over to the door and closed it.

Liam crawled back into bed and pulled the blanket up to his neck, suddenly feeling a bit cold. Just as his eyes closed, he heard it again—a slow creak.

He panicked, looking toward the bathroom. The door was open... *again.*

Liam started to feel that something was wrong. He slowly got near the door, trying to keep calm. A little scared, he peeked his head inside... AND — nothing.

No one was there.

Huffing, he closed the door again, this time making sure it latched properly and went back to bed.

But sleep was long gone. The blanket didn't keep him warm as the room felt colder, and Liam couldn't shake the feeling that he wasn't alone.

Then, he felt it. A presence on the other side of the bed.

Liam felt his heart pounding as he lay there, finding it difficult to breathe. Slowly, he rolled over, his eyes scanning the room. But there was nothing.

Right then, the bathroom door creaked open again. Determined to figure out why, Liam jumped out of bed and ran inside the bathroom. It seemed empty and dark, and then his eyes fell on the mirror in front of him.

That's when he saw.

A figure stood behind him, her face covered by long black hair. Her skin was pale and blue, and through a small gap in her hair, her eyes were glowing in the dark.

Liam tried to scream but no sound came out. He spun around in horror, but there was no one behind him. He dashed for the main door and tried to open it, but no luck. The door was locked. Liam was trapped inside the haunted room.

Before he could think of an escape the bathroom door flew open and every faucet inside started to run on their own.

Liam started pounding on the door, screaming for help. The door was still not budging when....

"Liaaam..."

It was a faint whisper, but it sent shivers down Liam's spine.

The whispering turned louder, heavier, echoing around the room.

Liam's head felt heavy, he could hear his heart pounding in his ear. The room started spinning, and Liam was soon engulfed by darkness.

The next day Liam found himself lying on the floor. Birds chirped outside and sunlight covered the room, showing that morning had arrived and the storm was over. For a moment, Liam was confused about why he was sleeping in front of the door, but it all came back.

He had hoped what he witnessed the previous night was just a bad dream but then Liam's eyes fell on the bathroom.

The door was wide open.

Frightened, he grabbed his things and ran out of the room. The door, which was jammed all night, now swung open easily.

He raced down to the lobby, towards the reception area. A new man stood behind the desk.

"Everything alright, sir?" the man asked. His voice was laced with concern.

Liam was breathless and couldn't form any words so he handed him the key to room 99, still trembling in fear. "Last night.... Another receptionist... he gave me this key."

"I am the only one who works here, sir." The man frowned as he replied.

"NO. There was another guy. He didn't talk much. He was wearing a cap... he gave me this key." Liam tried to reason but the man shook his head.

"That's not possible. Room 99 has been closed for years. No one should've given you that key," the man explained.

Liam's blood ran cold. He didn't ask any more questions and walked to the exit, his mind replaying the events of the night.

As he drove away from the hotel, Liam was certain of one thing: he had an encounter with a ghost.

After that, Liam never spent a night in a hotel again.

We'd Love to Hear from You!

Thank you for diving into these spooky tales with us! If you're enjoying the adventure so far, we'd greatly appreciate it if you could take a moment to leave a quick review on Amazon. Your feedback helps other readers discover this book and keeps the ghostly fun alive!

Simply visit: www.amazon.com/review/create-re-view?&asin=B0DHSTPGTR

Or scan the QR code below to go directly to the review page!

Your support means the world to us!

Chapter 7

The Unknown Terror

Sarah, a nurse who worked late shifts at the hospital, lived in a quiet apartment building. While the world sleeps, Sarah wakes up. And when she finally gets time to take a nap, a new day has already arrived. Her busy schedule left no time for her personal life and so Sarah had no one to greet when she returned home.

She was happy with her life, but soon everything was going to change... *for the worst.*

One cold, rainy night when Sarah's shift ended, the neighborhood was silent and the streets were empty. After a long and tiring day at work, she returned to her small, quiet apartment. The guard in the lobby greeted her and Sarah returned a smile before heading towards the elevator.

Once inside her apartment, she quickly freshened up and made dinner before collapsing into bed, exhausted, calling it a night.

The pitter-patter of rain created a cozy atmosphere for Sarah to fall asleep and the quiet hours made it perfect for her to doze off quickly... *until it wasn't peaceful and quiet anymore.*

Knock, knock, knock.

Sarah was drifting into sleep when she heard it. Low, but clear.

In the darkness there was silence. But somehow it sent a chill down her spine. Someone was outside her door, knocking.

Sarah checked the time. It was past midnight—who could it be at this hour? Alarmed, she got up and crept towards the door. With her one eye pressed against the peephole, she was surprised.

No one was outside her door.

Sarah thought against opening the door and checking the hallway.

"Maybe it was a dream." She thought, confused. There was an elderly couple and a woman on her floor and none of them seemed like pranksters.

She went back to bed and was about to get under the duvet when....

KNOCK, KNOCK, KNOCK!

The sound came again, much louder and more aggressive. Sarah, ready to catch the person red-handed, rushed and looked through the peephole. Again, there was no one.

But this time she opened the door a crack and peeked outside. The hallway was dark and empty.

"Whoever is doing this.... Quit harassing me. This isn't funny!" Sarah stated with rage into the empty air. All her life she had worked in the hospital and seen all sorts of things, so she wasn't easily scared.

But this? This was different. She could hear but see no one, and it was starting to frighten her.

The only sound was the soft hum of the wind outside. Locking the door, Sarah went back to bed, shaking off the unease. Lying still on her mattress, she wished for the knocking to stop.

And eventually, it did.

The next morning Sarah looked at her dull and gloomy reflection. She had only gotten an hour of sleep when the sunrays fell on her face.

Sarah didn't bother to eat and went to work.

That same night, the knocking came again. Weirdly, it only occurred when Sarah went to sleep and disappeared when she went to check.

Knock, knock, knock.

It happened the following night. And the next. And the next.

No one outside, just that eerie knocking growing louder, more insistent.

By the end of the week, Sarah found it hard to concentrate during her shift. She wasn't getting any sleep and was easily irritated by small things. However, it wasn't all because of the knocks.

Something strange was going on in her apartment.

Items were starting to disappear and then reappear in the wrong places. Her furniture shifted to new places, and – worst of all – she started to feel a presence.

A few nights back she'd heard a soft murmuring. Then two nights ago someone breathing on her face while she was asleep. Each time she opened her eyes the place was quiet and empty. No one was around, but it was enough to alarm her.

One day, Sarah's friend caught her dozing off during their shift. "You look more tired each passing day. Everything all, right?"

Finally, Sarah decided to confide in her friend, disclosing everything that had happened. Every terrible thing that destroyed her peace.

"I know this sounds ridiculous. But something is haunting me," Sarah's voice trembled as she recalled the events.

Once she was done sharing, her friend came up with an idea. "Maybe you should set up cameras. Those hidden ones that others cannot notice. Then you can see what's *really* happening."

Sarah agreed, her eyes bloodshot from exhaustion. At this point, she could even set up infrared cameras to catch ghosts... *if they were the ones haunting her.*

As planned, Sarah ordered a couple of hidden cameras. One was a toy for her bedroom—a stuffed bear with a hidden camera in its eyes. Another she got was a plant for the hallway, which had a camera concealed in the leaves.

Finally, she felt better knowing she was soon going to get some answers.

And so, another night came, and Sarah lay in bed...waiting... listening.

Just when she was starting to feel drowsy....

Knock, knock, knock.

Sarah squeezed her eyes shut, her heart racing. She hoped the cameras were catching whatever was happening, as the knocking only grew heavier. Eventually, she managed to fall asleep.

The next day, during her shift, Sarah excused herself and went to the washroom. She couldn't wait any longer, so she pulled out her phone and opened the camera footage from the hidden cameras.

Her hand trembled while she scrolled through.

Finally, saw it. There on the screen was a man standing in the middle of her room.

Sarah's breath caught in her throat.

Tall and scrawny, he walked casually around her apartment, almost as if he belonged there. He wandered from corner to corner, picking up her things and inspecting them.

What the man did next made her stomach drop. His eyes fell on the clock, and hurriedly he crawled underneath her bed, the place where he had been hiding since.... Forever.

Sarah's blood ran cold. How could this man get inside her room? Since when had he been there?

She had been living with this stranger in her home without knowing. She quickly rewound the footage, needing to know how this man got in. And then she saw something that made her stomach twist in knots.

The knocking from the previous night. There was no one at the door in the footage.

The noise... all this time—it was coming from... inside.

Sarah paused the video, her hands shaking. Slowly, she rewound it, this time paying close attention to the knocking.

It was coming from under her bed.

Her heart raced as she watched in horror. It was the man... underneath her bed, knocking on the wooden frame from below. This entire time, he made Sarah feel restless without even appearing before her.

Panic surged through her. Frightened, Sarah called the police. They caught the man hiding under the bed, waiting for her to return home, *like always.*

The man was in handcuffs when the officers pulled him outside the apartment. He creepily smiled at Sarah, who felt disgusted by it.

When he was asked when and how he'd gotten inside, his answer sent a final chill down Sarah's spine.

"The door was left unlocked one night," he chuckled, his voice evil. "I walked right in. Been living here ever since."

Sarah was horrified. She had made a grave mistake. And she had no clue about it until then.

Before getting dragged inside the car, the stranger leaned toward her, whispering, "Always lock your doors. Not everyone is as nice as me."

After that incident, Sarah moved to a new apartment that was in a secure neighborhood. She installed cameras, double locks, and everything to feel safe.

However, every night, before going to bed, she couldn't help but check underneath the bed. Because no matter what she did or how secure her new place was, Sarah would always feel like someone might be hiding... just waiting for her to close her eyes.

Chapter 8

MAMA

Mary and Jack were excited for the birth of their first child. They were soon going to be parents and had spent months preparing the nursery.

But life is cruel sometimes.

The baby became a little angel in heaven shortly after birth.

Struck with tragedy, a heartbroken Mary couldn't bear to set foot in the nursery again. Her husband Jack, grieving, tried to cheer up his wife but nothing seemed to bring them comfort.

Days passed, and while Jack drowned himself in work, Mary slipped deeper into despair. Time in the house went by but the couple was stuck in the cruel past.

However, something strange soon occurred in their life on one eventful night.

The house was dark and quiet. Mary and Jack were asleep when...

"Mama... Mama...!!"

Mary woke up, sitting bolt upright in bed. Heartbroken by her dream, she glanced at Jack who was sound asleep. She shook her head and was about to lay down but then, she heard it again.

"Mama...." Followed by a soft cry. That of a baby.

Her baby? Mary felt her heart pounding in her chest. She wasn't dreaming. She really did hear something – barely audible but unmistakable.

The sound was coming from the nursery.

Without thinking, Mary threw the covers off and rushed down the hall. Her heart filled with hope and her feet moved without missing a beat.

The door to the nursery room was ajar. Mary hesitated a bit. She hadn't set foot here since... she couldn't remember for how many days.

The room had been empty. But not anymore. Mary's child was calling out for her.

She flung open the door.

The room was exactly as they had left it and the crib, sitting in the corner, wasn't empty.

Mary froze. Her eyes couldn't believe what she was seeing. However, she was overjoyed at the sight.

The baby was lying there, tiny and perfect, smiling up at her, just like the day she was born. Mary's breath caught in her throat. This felt too real.

Tears welled in Mary's eyes as she saw the baby struggling to hold up her tiny hands in the air. It was longing for a mother's love.

And Mary didn't want to waste any more time.

She scooped her baby into her arms, goosebumps spread across her body as she felt the temperature of the room drop a little. Even so, in the coldness, Mary felt alive for the first time in weeks.

That fateful night, Mary stayed in the nursery, cradling her baby until morning.

When she informed Jack about the miracle that occurred, his heart sank. Mary was not making any sense and he felt she was slowly starting to lose her mind.

Until he witnessed the same.

That same night, the baby started crying for *'Mama,'* and a strange pull brought Mary towards the crib. As she carried her baby in her arms and sang a lullaby, Jack's blood ran cold.

They were able to see their dead child. Unlike Mary, Jack believed in spirits and the afterlife, and somehow, he knew this wasn't their baby.

He tried to set his foot inside the room and pull Mary away to the safety of his arms but he couldn't. The room didn't want Jack anywhere near it so he helplessly and hopelessly watched his wife talking and playing with the child.

He hoped for the nightmare to end quickly.

But it didn't. The next night, the same thing happened. And the night after that.

Every night, the couple heard the baby's voice calling out —"Mama"—and each time it happened, Mary would rush to the nursery to find her baby waiting for her.

Jack did try to reason with his wife. "Mary, you need to stop this. Whatever we are seeing...it's not real." But Mary ignored his words each time. "It is. I can feel it and a mother's intuition doesn't lie."

No one could separate her and her child anymore.

Jack began to worry.

Mary had stopped leaving the house, stopped eating properly, and was getting paler and thinner each passing day. Jack knew she was starting to pay the price for talking to the dead. Why couldn't Mary see that?

While Mary saw this as a blessing... a miracle, Jack saw something else—something darker.

His wife's energy was draining away and so was her will to see reality. Her health was deteriorating slowly.

Desperate, Jack reached out to a priest, hoping to put an end to this unnatural routine. The priest listened to his story with a grave look.

"This is a bad omen," the priest warned. "You need to stop your wife, otherwise, you might lose her as well."

The warning lingered in his head as Jack rushed home. And what he saw made his eyes grow big in disbelief.

There in the living room was Mary sitting on a couch and knitting tiny clothes. For the baby. She had already completed making a few and was sewing a baby sweater while humming a soft tune.

Jack's skin crawled as he watched her. Clothes were lying everywhere around her and Mary was happily stitching some more.

"Jack! Look..." Mary held up a small red sweater, noticing her husband. "Isn't this perfect for our baby? Or do you think it's too big?"

Her eyes had a strange glow and her face had a sweet smile.

Jack's heart sank. He knelt in front of her, gently taking her hands in his. "Mary," he whispered. "Our baby is gone. It's just you and me."

Mary's eyes widened and she snatched her hand back. "No! You are lying. Every night I hold my baby in my arms. You saw it too."

Sighing, Jack pulled out his phone. This was the last thing he wanted to do.

He scrolled through his gallery and showed his wife the pictures of the last day they spent with their baby.

"Mary, look. This is the truth," Jack said, his voice cracking.

As if reality finally hit her, Mary stared at the picture, her face slowly turning into a frown and then... she finally broke down.

Jack held her in his arms and the couple shared their tragedy... crying, sobbing for hours.

That night they lay in bed, both exhausted from facing the truth. And just as they were about to drift off, they heard it again.

"Mama.... Mama..."

Mary tensed, taken aback. She wanted to get up, to run to the nursery, but Jack held her back. "No," he pleaded. "Please don't."

"MAMA.... MAMA!"

The voice grew louder, more insistent.

Mary covered her ears in agony. She couldn't take it anymore.

"MAMAAAA......MAMAAAA!!!"

The voice, filled with rage, started to change. The voice that was once sweet and soft now sounded heavy and dark.

It was no longer a baby crying. A demonic voice had taken over.

The couple huddled together, terrified, as the walls started to vibrate and the house seemed to shake violently.

Objects began to fly across the room and the doors flung open. The place was tearing itself down but Mary and Jack stayed silent, shivering in each other's arms.

And then, as suddenly as it had begun, the voice stopped. And so did the madness.

Silence filled the house. After what felt like hours, Mary and Jack tiptoed to the nursery door, but saw no one in there. The baby was gone. Mary felt a stab in her heart but Jack was relieved.

That was the last time they ever heard the voice.

Soon after that, Mary began to recover. Her health slowly got better but the incident of that night still haunted their dreams.

A few months later they shifted to a new house, to start afresh with a new memory. The new home did bring a new beginning in their life as a year later, they welcomed a baby boy.

And this time, the baby was born healthy and full of life, and soon grew to fit into the clothes Mary had once knitted. *So perfectly as if they were originally made for him.*

Chapter 9

The Tale of Hanako

Anna and her family had just moved to Japan. Her father's job brought the family to this unfamiliar, beautiful country and although everything was new to Anna, she was excited.

Her cheerful, outgoing personality helped her to blend in the crowd easily so Anna never found it difficult to make friends. Instead, she was thrilled about her new school! *Hope everyone accepts me*; she thought and slept early because tomorrow was going to be her first day at the school.

Finally, the day arrived for Anna. Her class teacher introduced her to the students. "Class, this is Anna. She just moved here from California and I'm sure you will all help her feel welcome."

The teacher then gestured for Anna to introduce herself. Although she was a little nervous, Anna smiled and gave a small bow. "Hello, my name is Anna! I am excited to be here and I look forward to getting to know all of you."

Her whole introduction was in Japanese, which Anna had been learning for the past few weeks. She wanted to make a good impression on her first day since she knew that as an outsider, it would be tough for her to make friends.

However, she was determined. And thankfully her efforts paid off.

The room was quiet for a moment, and then they broke into applause. Most of her classmates appreciated her broken Japanese and so did Anna's teacher, who patted her shoulder.

However, amidst the praise, Anna failed to notice the dislike towards her.

In the back of the class, two girls, Sakura and Yuki, shared a look of distaste while everyone else was excited to have a foreign student among them.

"What's so great about her? She is an attention-seeker." Sakura seethed, her eyes focused on Anna.

Yuki, on the other hand, giggled. She knew very well that when Sakura showed irritation toward someone it meant she has taken an interest in that person. *A special kind of interest.*

"What do you have in mind?" Yuki asked. Sakura's eyes shone with mischief as she spoke, "Let's give her a tour during lunchtime. One that she will never forget."

With a smirk, both of them were now eager for the lunch break.

During lunch break the two girls approached Anna, who was clueless about their true motive.

"Hi, I am Sakura and this is Yuki. We just wanted to tell you that your Japanese skills were amazing for a beginner." In her most sweet voice, Sakura cheered. Yuki wore a big smile on her face.

Anna's eyes lit up. She thanked them politely.

"Do you want a tour of the school? We can show you around." Sakura suggested, and predictably, Anna happily agreed to the idea.

She was excited to explore and thought that it was her chance to make new friends.

Their classroom was on the first floor, so the trio went up to the 2nd floor. Sakura and Yuki led Anna through the busy hallways, pointing out labs and the gym area.

Then came the 3rd floor. Strangely, Anna noticed that both Sakura and Yuki were hyper-excited when they climbed up to the floor.

Poor Anna thought maybe they were usually that cheerful. *If only she knew the truth.*

The floor was strangely quiet.

"Why is it empty?" Anna asked, noticing the lack of students and teachers.

"The seniors have gone to a sports event. This is their floor," explained Yuki, innocently.

But Anna didn't like the silence. She was cheerful and outgoing but, just like everyone, she got scared too. And she was scared of the empty hallway.

Something about it felt strange....

"We should head back now." Anna tried to escape, but failed.

Sakura held her arm. "Wait! Why don't we say hello to Hanako-San?"

Confused, Anna stopped in her tracks and asked, "Who is Hanako-San?"

"She's a shy girl. And also, an outsider... just like you." Anna heard Yuki say and didn't like the way she mentioned 'outsider.' It almost felt like a taunt. Or perhaps, she was so scared that everything about her surroundings started to bother her.

"She used to live in the U.S. but unlike you, she had a hard time adjusting here. Now, she has no friend and eats her lunch inside the bathroom.... *all alone*." Sakura added, her face morphed into sadness.

Anna felt bad for this Hanako girl. No matter the ethnicity, no one should go through an experience like this. Anna wanted to befriend her. "We should invite her to eat with us."

Sakura and Yuki burst out into laughter. Anna was more innocent than they thought... or rather, dumb.

"Yes, we should." The two girls then led Anna to the girl's bathroom where supposedly this Hanako girl was having her lunch.

Before going in, Sakura stopped Anna.

Anna frowned. She was slowly getting irritated by the manhandling. "As I said, Hanako is a shy girl so you need to be persistent. Go to the third stall, knock three times, and say, *'Are you there, Hanako-san?'* She will like that."

Sakura's instructions were strangely precise and weird.

Anna hesitated. This seemed odd. But maybe this was a type of Japanese greeting she had no clue about. Anna didn't ask any questions. Besides, how bad could it be to knock on a bathroom door?

Unfortunately, what Anna didn't know was that according to an urban Japanese legend, Hanako-san is rumored to be a bathroom ghost who had died during WWII. If someone goes to a third-floor bathroom, knocks on the 3rd stall 3 times, and asks "Are you there, Hanako-san?" the ghost will reply and then they have to quickly exit the place or she will drag the person with her into the toilet from where no one can return.

Being new to the country, Anna had no clue about the scary legend so she did what she was asked.

Standing in front of the door, Anna looked back, feeling uneasy, but Sakura and Yuki gestured for her to knock quickly.

So, Anna did it.

She knocked once.

Twice.

Finally, three times. "Are you there, Hanako-San?"

No answer.

Anna waited but nothing.

She turned back around to tell the girls, but just as she opened her mouth, the bathroom door slammed shut behind her with a loud **BANG.**

Her eyes widened. Anna ran to the door and tried to pull it open. "Hey, open the door!" she yelled.

Sakura and Yuki were laughing from the other side. The sound was pure evil and cruel.

"Have fun!" they mocked, their footsteps fading as they left Anna inside, trapped.... And all alone.

"This isn't funny! Please don't leave me here!!" Anna cried for help but she knew no one would be able to hear her as the floor was empty.

Anna's heart was pounding. She looked back at the bathroom she was trapped in. Slowly, she walked to the third stall and pushed open the door. The stall was empty.

They had pranked her; Anna felt miserable.

She was quick to trust them and all they did was make a fool out of her. Somehow, this made her angry. Anna was afraid of the dark and isolation, and she had to face both her fears now.

It's just a bathroom. There are people in this building. No need to be scared. She glanced back at the empty stalls and the lights flickered. Okay, maybe it was a little scary.

Anna tried to remind herself that it was morning outside, but the eerie silence of the empty floor made her heart beat faster. She could feel something... *or someone watching her.*

Maybe my mind is playing tricks on me; she thought.

Suddenly, the lights flickered more intensely, and Anna tried to open the door again, fear overtaking her senses. "Someone, please help!"

After what felt like an hour, a teacher, who was doing her rounds, heard a voice yelling from inside the bathroom and unlocked the door.

"What are you doing here?" the teacher asked, bewildered.

Anna, shaken and dumbfounded, came up with a lie about getting lost. The teacher gave her a strange look but led her back to class.

She had missed two periods and had to get an earful from the teachers about discipline and time management. Anna couldn't raise her head, feeling embarrassed and humiliated.

But she had learnt her lesson. Sakura and Yuki were grinning at her as Anna walked past them.

She wanted nothing more to do with those two troublemakers. After that, for the rest of the day, Anna avoided them.

"I knew it. There are no such things as ghosts. Look at her. She came back all well." Sakura said, somewhat bitter about Anna's returning unharmed.

"I think it was all a rumor," Yuki added.

Later that day, as school ended, Sakura stayed back to return some books she borrowed. After coming back from the library, she saw that Yuki was waiting for her in the classroom. Everyone had already gone home and they were the only ones left.

Suddenly, Sakura realized she needed to use the bathroom. She asked Yuki to follow her but unfortunately, the guard had already locked the ones on their floor. Even the second floor was inaccessible.

Left with no choice, Sakura and Yuki made their way up to the 3rd floor. As they entered the empty bathroom, Sakura chuckled, remembering how they tricked Anna.

"What a dumb girl," she said to Yuki, who was quiet this whole time. She mimicked the way Anna walked and talked. And on a whim, Sakura knocked on the 3rd stall 3 times, while mimicking the way Anna asked --- 'Are you there, Hanako-San?'

"How foolish of her." Laughing, Sakura then went inside the 2nd stall to take care of her business.

She was done and ready to walk out when her phone buzzed. She saw a message from Yuki: *Sorry, I had to leave early. My grandparents are here to visit.*

Sakura froze. Her blood ran cold after reading the message again. She stared at the bathroom door. If Yuki was already home... who was waiting outside for her?

A cold chill ran down her spine.

From the small gap under her door, she noticed the bathroom was empty. No one was there except for her.

Or so she thought.

Her eyes fell on the stall beside her and saw a pair of shoes. **Someone was in the third stall.**

Sakura started trembling in fear. She ran out and tried to get away but fate had something else for her.

The door was locked. Earlier, one of the guards came and locked the door from outside, not knowing that someone was still there.

Sakura banged on the door, her heart pounding in her chest.

Suddenly, the lights flickered and a faint whisper came from inside the 3rd stall. "You called me... Sakura-San."

The lights went out and Sakura could feel a presence behind her.

Scared for her life, she gasped and spun around. Her body froze when she saw it....

There, in the dark, stood Hanako, with her small, pale figure, and hollow, black eyes.

"I've been waiting.... for you," Hanako dragged her words and smiled, showing her rotten, yellow teeth.

Sakura screamed, banging on the door, but she was doomed. Hanako floated closer, and in the empty hallway and vacant building, Sakura's scream echoed but no one came to help her.

The next morning, when the guard came and opened the lock, no one was inside.

Sakura was gone. No one saw her again. No one knew what happened to her, but Yuki, having a weird feeling, transferred to another school.

However, she was never quite the same. She couldn't shake the uneasiness in her heart... as if someone was watching... *waiting for her*.

Chapter 10
A Wish Fulfilled

It all started when Eli's grandma came to live with them. The last time Eli had seen his grandma was when he was a baby. He couldn't remember much about the days they spent together, but Eli remembered one thing about his grandmother.

She wasn't just any grandmother. She had superpowers - she could see ghosts.

Eli had always been fascinated by ghosts. He loved the thrill of a good ghost story, the ones that made the hair on the back of his neck stand up. On the other hand, his parents weren't such strong believers. They always said that there's no such thing as ghosts.

But Eli knew better. Thus, he was beyond excited when he heard his grandmother was coming to stay with them for a week.

The grandma didn't look like someone who could see ghosts all the time. When she arrived, she looked like a normal grandma, kind and sweet.

Eli wondered if this was the same person who dealt with scary stuff. "Do you *really* see ghosts, Grandma?" Eli asked her one night, wanting to hear some scary bedtime stories.

His grandmother smiled. "I don't just see them – I *sense* them, my child."

Eli's eyes grew wide. They were glowing.

"Are they scary? Like the ones in books?"

Grandma laughed a little. Eli's excitement was new to her. "Some are," she replied. "But not all of them are scary."

"In movies, ghosts are always shown living in our world. Don't they have their own world to live in? Why live among humans?" Eli grew confused as he remembered a scene from the movie his parents were watching a few days ago.

He shuddered in fear when the ghost popped out of nowhere and scared the hell out of the family in the movie.

"You see Eli, ghosts have some wishes they want to fulfill, something they couldn't do when they were alive. That's why they stay back. Just like you and me, they too have motives. It all depends on their story. And sometimes they just need a little help from humans to achieve that," grandma said, her voice soft but serious.

"Then did you help any ghost, grandma?" Eli asked, but she only smiled. The kind that meant that she had a story to tell but it was for another time.

His grandma had a way of making even the spookiest things sound kind of... fun.

The next day, Eli took his grandma on a walk around the neighborhood. They visited places like Eli's favorite park, the corner store where he liked to buy candy, and the big oak tree he liked to sleep under.

As the sun began to set, they were wandering around the abandoned part of the town. Eli hesitated taking another step. "Let's head back, grandma. Mom and Dad told me not to be around this part. They said it was dangerous," Eli said, glancing at the run-down buildings and empty streets.

Grandma nodded, not wanting to put Eli in a tight spot. He was already growing nervous. "Someday you have to face your fear, Eli. But don't worry, the time hasn't come yet," she said, playfully pinching his cheeks.

With grandma, even in the scariest places, Eli didn't feel any fear. And one day he would be as brave as his grandma; Eli promised himself.

They were walking back to their neighborhood when they came across a big playground. Eli spotted a boy on the swing, all alone, swaying back and forth.

Eli recognized the boy. He lived in the neighborhood but had no friends.

"That's Noah," Eli said in a whisper. "There are some bad rumors about his parents.... I don't know too well... but people here don't like them nor do they chat with them."

"What about Noah? Doesn't he have any friends?" Grandma enquired, studying the boy.

"He is always by himself. No kid in the block plays or talk with him." Eli replied, feeling a bit ashamed as he was one of those kids who ignored Noah.

"He looks lonely. Why don't you go and play with him?" Grandma suggested.

Eli hesitated. "I don't know. We've never talked before."

Grandma gave him a gentle nudge. "Everyone needs a friend Eli, and maybe, Noah will like your company."

"You think so?" Eli asked.

"I know so." Grandma smiled and ushered him to go play with Noah.

Eli took a deep breath and approached the boy. "Hey, Noah. Want to play?"

Noah didn't look up at first but when Eli introduced himself and said he wanted them to be friends, Noah lifted his head.

Eli noticed how thin and fragile Noah looked. But then, a smile spread across his pale face—a smile that made Eli's heart warm.

"I'd love that," Noah replied, his voice barely audible.

For the next hour, the two boys ran around the playground while grandma sat on a nearby bench and watched. They played tag and hide-n-seek, had a great time on the swings, and laughed so hard their sides hurt.

Eli couldn't believe he had ignored Noah all this time. *He was so fun!*

Soon they grew tired and sat on the ground, catching their breath. Noah turned to Eli and said, "This is the first time anyone played with me. I had so much fun. Thanks, Eli!" His face was no longer pale. It glowed in the dark with joy and satisfaction.

"I had fun too and I am sorry I ignored you all this time." Eli apologized. "Let's do this again."

Noah smiled but didn't say anything. Instead, he stood up and waved goodbye, heading back toward the empty streets.

However, before he disappeared, Noah turned back and expressed his gratitude to Eli one more time. Somehow this one felt strange to Eli. It seemed like no one had ever been kind to him before.

Eli was happy he listened to his grandma. On their way home, Grandma looked down at Eli with a soft smile and said, "You did a good thing. That kid will remember it forever."

Eli shrugged, though he felt proud. "I'm glad I listened to you. That was fun." He chirped.

As they were near their house, they met an elderly woman from the neighborhood. She was a nosy lady who knew everyone's business and loved to gossip. "I see you are showing your grandma around. Where are you guys coming from?" she asked and although Eli didn't like her prying, he wasn't a rude kid.

So, he replied that they were just coming from the abandoned neighborhood. This surprised the elderly woman and she warned Eli not to go there by himself.

She then turned toward Eli's grandma and said, "That part of town is just bad news. Although I am sorry for what happened to Noah's parents."

Eli wasn't rude, nor did he interrupt when elders were talking. But the mention of Noah caught his interest. "Why? What happened to Noah's parents?" His face grew serious.

"Not his parents but the kid himself. He passed away about a month ago. Since then, his parents have gone mad with grief...." The woman paused and shook her head.

A tragedy had struck the family; one Eli wasn't aware of.

The elderly woman took her leave, and Eli turned to grandma, his eyes full of pain and sadness.

"Is that true grandma? Did you know that Noah was a ghost all along?" Eli's voice trembled in disbelief.

Grandma nodded. Eli was confused. *Why didn't grandma tell him that? Why did she let him play with a ghost?*

"What was he doing in the playground then?" Eli asked.

"Remember what I told you the previous night, Eli? About ghosts with wishes to fulfill? Well, Noah had a wish as well. He wanted to play with someone... to feel what it would be like to have a friend. He never had the chance when he was alive but today for you, he felt alive.... When he wasn't." For a kid Eli's age, grandma's words were a lot to process but he knew one thing.

Noah meant no harm.

Eli's mind raced. He had spent the whole afternoon playing with a ghost, but he didn't feel scared. In fact, it made him feel good.

"Why didn't you tell me?" he asked.

Grandma chuckled softly and asked, "Would you have played with him the same way after knowing he was a ghost?" Eli shook his head. He knew Noah wouldn't have harmed him in any way but still, he was afraid of ghosts.

Eli thought about it and realized grandma was right. If he had known, he probably would have run away. And then would have missed such an amazing time playing with Noah.

Before they reached home, grandma took off her necklace—a small, silver chain she always wore—and made Eli wear it.

"This will keep you safe," she said. "Just like it kept me all this time. You're brave, Eli. You saw what others couldn't, and you weren't afraid."

Eli smiled, feeling anxious and excited at the same time. "Does that mean I will see more ghosts from now?"

"Perhaps. But now you know, not all ghosts are something to be afraid of." Grandma winked.

Eli never told anyone about his day with the ghost boy. It was his and grandma's little secret.

And from then on, Eli always made sure to look twice, just in case someone else needed his help.

Chapter 11

The Scary Pumpkin Patch

On a chilly and spooky day, it was that time of the year again. Halloween returned, and so did the classic trick-or-treat.

Kids were out for their annual candy hunt, and among those kids was a group of four. Dressed in their Halloween costumes, Jacob, Amy, Leon, and Ivy wandered from house to house, their candy baskets getting heavier for their entertaining performance.

Jacob, the eldest of the group, was dressed as Jack Sparrow, his sword clinking against his leg. Amy, with her black dress and pale makeup, dolled up as Wednesday Addams; a bored look on her face. Leon, who was a fan of cool superheroes, proudly wore his Spiderman suit... five years in a row. And Ivy, who was always a little nerdier than the others, had donned her Hermione costume, proudly swaying her wand.

"Is that a real knife?" Leon pointed out; his eyes wide at the sharp object on Jacob's costume. Jacob nodded as he carried the weapon, wanting to feel like a real pirate of the sea.

The day was going well – each of their baskets was filled to the brim. Cookies, candies, and chocolates were piled up. As the sky darkened, the kids decided to head back.

They lost their bearings while going around collecting treats and when they realized, Jacob and the others found themselves in the quieter part of the town. All around there were a few abandoned houses with no sign of Halloween decoration outside.

The streets were lined with overgrown hedges that looked like they had not been taken care of in a long time.

"Let's go home," Ivy suggested as they neared the outskirts of town. The sun was setting and they weren't familiar with this part of town.

Jacob and the others agreed that it was best if they walked out of there. The kids then started their journey towards their neighborhood when suddenly they found themselves passing by the old and abandoned pumpkin patch.

The group felt uneasy. They were in a part of town people rarely visited, and for good reason. Ivy glanced nervously at the old, rusted gate that stood tall ahead of them. Beyond it lay the pumpkin patch — a place where no one ever went.

"That's the haunted pumpkin patch," Amy said, her voice trembling. "We really shouldn't be here."

Before they could turn back, a voice broke through the chilly air.

"Well... well, look who it is!" Liam and his gang appeared, laughing. "If not the *Infamous* Four." Nothing was funny about Liam's remark but the rest of his group, dressed as zombies, laughed out loud as if they had heard the best joke of the year.

Liam, the town's well-known troublemaker and the school bully, was wearing a Dracula costume. His fangs were too big for his mouth and he looked ridiculous but Jacob and his friends knew better than to laugh. No one laughed at Liam. If you did, you would be in grave danger.

"Afraid of a few pumpkins, are you?" Liam mocked, his eyes gleaming with mischief.

"We are not! Now leave us alone," Jacob said, though his voice lacked its usual confidence.

"Then prove it," Liam grinned, his eyes narrowing. "I bet you can't spend five minutes in that pumpkin patch. If you do, we'll leave you alone for good."

Jacob hesitated. It was a tempting offer. Liam and his gang had been tormenting them for months. A chance to make it stop was hard to resist.

"Fine," Jacob agreed, trying to appear braver than he felt. "We will go in. But you have to come too."

Liam shrugged and asked Jacob to lead the way, "After you."

The tall and tarnished gate had a big red sign – STAY AWAY – hanging crookedly. But it was too late for the kids to obey.

The group walked inside after they pushed open the gates. A loud, creaking sound startled Jacob and his friends while Liam and his group laughed at their cowardly display.

Suddenly, a murder of crows erupted from the trees, their harsh cawing echoing through the patch. Ivy and Amy held each other's hands, their hearts beating loudly. Leon was behind Jacob, following him closely, scared and anxious. The air inside the patch was colder, and the ground seemed to shift beneath their feet.

As they walked further in, something felt wrong. There were no pumpkins, no vines, nothing but dirt. Ivy tugged on Jacob's sleeve. "This is a bad idea. Let's go," she whispered.

But before anyone could move, the ground beneath them trembled. Out of nowhere, pumpkins erupted from underneath, their vines wriggling like snakes. The kids screamed as the vines shot toward their feet, binding them in place. Liam, for all his brave facade, was screaming the loudest of all.

Amy and Ivy screamed, Leon struggled, but the vines only tightened.

Trapped and helpless, the kids started to shout for help.

From the darkness, a low, sinister laugh echoed. The pumpkins shifted, stepping aside and making way for a massive figure—a giant pumpkin head with glowing eyes and a toothy, evil grin. Its voice was deep and frightening. "A group of intruders. What a sight to behold!"

The other pumpkin heads laughed and howled at their leader's words while the kids shuddered in fear. Never in their life had they seen a pumpkin talk and move... and such a giant one too.

Jacob, struggling against the vines, hated to see his friends at its mercy. "What do you want from us? Leave us alone!" He shouted.

The pumpkin head grinned wider, its carved face illuminated by an eerie orange glow. "Oh, I do need something from you. I've been trapped here for centuries. But tonight, I'll be free. I need a body – a human body for my head. And one of you will give it to me."

The children gasped in horror. *There is no escape now*, they thought and started sobbing.

The pumpkin's roots pulled them tighter, the vines inching higher up their legs. Liam, for once, realized his mistake – he had done something he shouldn't have.

Jacob's mind raced. He needed to do something, anything, to save his friends. As the pumpkin head began inspecting them, an idea popped up in his head.

While the pumpkin was distracted circling the other kids, Jacob gathered some dirt in his hand.

He waited, his heart pounding in his chest until the pumpkin head was looming over him. "Come closer. If you want a body, you need to inspect us properly." He demanded. The giant pumpkin head leaned in closer.

At that moment, Jacob threw the dirt into its glowing eyes.

"Aarrrghhh!!!" The pumpkin roared in pain, its minions running to help.

In the chaos, Jacob pulled out the real knife he had brought with him as part of his pirate costume. He quickly slashed through the vines holding him, then moved to free his friends.

"Run!" Jacob shouted. They all sprinted toward the gate.

The giant pumpkin thundered and thrashed wildly. But it was too late. The kids were able to escape him and his scary pumpkin patch.

They slammed the gate shut behind them and scurried away to safety. Night had arrived and the kids stopped a few blocks away, panting heavily, holding their knees.

That's when Liam's group noticed something strange.

Liam was nowhere to be seen. "Where's Liam?" one of the friends asked, his zombie makeup now drenched in sweat and dirt.

The group, eyes wide with fear, realized something bad had happened to Liam.

"We have to go back," Jacob muttered, but no one else nodded their head.

They all were too tired and scared... afraid of what those pumpkins might do if they got caught again.

"No way. I can't risk my life. We barely made it outside," one of Liam's friends spoke while the others agreed with him.

Liam was a jerk to all; friends or not.

"He is right. Let's get out of here and then call the police." Leon suggested but Liam's group was far too afraid to get involved. They all ran away leaving behind Jacob and his friends... but most of all, Liam... in that scary pumpkin patch.

However, Jacob couldn't leave Liam behind, not even someone as cruel as him. "What if it's too late? He is a kid just like us. Yes, he is bad and has done some cruel things but I bet he is as scared as you and me now." He said to his friends, who kept quiet.

Jacob was right. They weren't as cruel as Liam... or his *so-called* friends.

"You are right." Ivy finally agreed. "Plus, it's Halloween. My mom says festivals should be spent with everyone. That's where the real joy and happiness lies."

"Yes. No one deserves to be left behind on Halloween," Amy said and soon they were all determined to help Liam.

Reluctantly, but together, they stepped into the pumpkin patch. The gate opened with a loud, creaking sound and once again they came face to face with the small, evil pumpkins.

As if they were waiting for the kids.

"You're all fools to come back here," one of them hissed wickedly.

The kids were holding each other's hands and thus this time they felt less scared.

"Where's Liam?" Jacob demanded, his face serious.

The pumpkins laughed together but when Jacob took out his knife and threatened to cut them into pieces, they all cowered.

The boy was in no mood for chatting and wasting time.

"The master took him underground for the sacrifice ritual," the pumpkins said in unison.

The group raced toward an underground tunnel, dark and cold. Truth be told, the kids were scared for their life but then they looked at each other, determined to put an end to all this.

With each other's help, Jacob and his friends climbed down carefully. Stepping on the ground, they patted their clothes and noticed a terrified Liam, tied to a rock, crying as the giant pumpkin head was busy preparing a bubbling pot of strange liquid.

"You're back!" the giant pumpkin seethed in anger. "But too late. Soon, I'll have a body, and your friend will be no more." His laughter echoed in the darkness.

But Jacob had one last idea. "Wait!" he shouted. "If you want to be human you need to know the rules of the human world. Do you?"

The pumpkin hesitated. "What rules?"

Jacob grinned. "To live in the human world the first rule is to close your eyes and hold your breath. Like this."

Jacob nudged his friends who got the clue. They all closed their eyes and held their breath showing they all could do it.

"Now it's your turn. If you can't, I'm sorry to say you won't be able to live among us," Jacob said, his tone challenging.

The pumpkin, eager to live as a human, quickly closed its eyes.

That was all Jacob needed. He and his friends rushed forward, shoving the giant pumpkin head into the bubbling pot.

The creature screamed, thrashing around as it slowly melted into the liquid, its eerie glow fading away.

The kids untied Liam in a hurry and climbed out of the passage. With the giant pumpkin gone, the patch returned to normal. The small pumpkins withered and slowly faded away and the once-scary place now seemed like any other ordinary field.

Liam was filled with guilt and remorse. He turned to Jacob, his face filled with gratitude. "Thank you... and I'm truly sorry," he whispered.

Jacob smiled. "Just remember your promise. No more bullying. Let's help each other in need from now on."

Liam nodded, having learned his lesson. Together, they all left the patch and the horrors behind them. But none of them would ever forget the haunted pumpkin patch, and the night it almost claimed a body.

Chapter 12

A Scary Lesson

B rian was the well-known troublemaker in his class. He bullied other students and even pulled pranks on teachers. No one was safe from his mischievous acts. And the best part? He always got away with it. His parents were good friends with the principal, so Brian never faced any consequences. It made him bolder, crueler.

But not for long. Soon Brian would learn his lesson... the hard way.

On one bright, autumn day, Brian pulled off what he thought was one of his best tricks yet. During math class, as the teacher was scribbling formulas on the board, Brian launched a paper airplane that glided smoothly across the room and hit the teacher right in the back of his head.

He stifled a laugh when the teacher turned around, fuming with rage. "Who threw this?" he asked, picking up the crumpled piece of paper with equations written on it.

Brian was waiting for this. He raised his hand and pointed at Ben, who was sitting right in front of him.

"I saw him doing it!" Brian shouted, surprising Ben, who had no idea what he had done.

However, the teacher was in no mood to listen. Ben pleaded that it wasn't him who threw the plane but when his bag was searched Ben's eyes widened in shock, and his face turned red.

Dozens of paper planes were pulled out of his bag. Ben had no clue how they got there but when he saw Brian smirking, he knew who was behind it.

Of course, it was none other than Brian the bully, Ben thought and tried to protest but no one would believe him. Brian watched smugly as Ben was sent to stand in the hallway, humiliated.

The following week, things got worse. Brian moved on to his next victim; this time a girl named Emily.

Brian had been chewing gum all day and when no one looked he sneakily stuck the gum in Emily's braided hair. He was evil enough to stick it on the top of her head.

When Emily found the wad of gum firmly sitting on the crown of her head, she burst into tears. Her friends tried to reassure her and stated some remedies to remove it but nothing calmed her down.

When she came to school the next day, the class was horrified. The hair was tangled together so Emily had to shave her head. There was a golf ball-sized patch of hair missing on her head and she had to wear a hat to hide her embarrassment.

"How on earth did a gum get stuck in my hair?" Brian heard Emily asking her friends in distress and he just snickered to himself. Another victory.

Later that day, when the cafeteria was buzzing with kids, Brian's eyes fell on his next target; a chubby, lone kid in his class who had his plate full of lunch. Brian smirked, making his way towards the oblivious kid.

"You're too fat to eat it." He snatched the food away and continued, "Go on a one-week diet."

The kid, hurt and humiliated, cowered away and ran from the cafeteria, leaving his lunch with Brian.

Brian loved dominating his classmates, as it made him feel superior. Someone with power... and he had enough of it.

The kids were afraid of him and the teachers were afraid of his parents. Brian had everyone under his control.

One day, Brian noticed Max, a boy in his class, showing off an old phone to some friends. It wasn't just any phone—it was an old, vintage model that looked expensive and timeless, like something straight out of a spy movie.

What Brian sees, Brian wants. And right now, he wanted Max's phone.

Max mentioned it had been a gift from his grandfather before he passed away. However, the words had no impact on Brian. He *needed* that phone. So, he came up with a plan.

Later that day, while everyone was at gym class, Brian snuck into Max's bag and stole the phone. He hid it in his locker, smiling and proud of himself.

By the time gym was over, the phone was gone, and Max was too afraid to tell anyone. He searched everywhere but he couldn't find it.

The boy was devastated as he knew he'd get in trouble for bringing it to school in the first place. There was no way he could tell his teachers.

Max never stood a chance. Brian knew about the school's no-phone policy and he was on cloud nine. No one would ever find out that the phone was stolen – it was his now.

Back home, his parents were out and his sister was busy studying in her room so Brian went to his room and locked the door. The place was a mess but he didn't care. He was too busy checking out his prize.

He turned on the phone and swiped it open. However, he frowned, noticing something weird.

Strangely, the phone had no pictures, no apps, no contacts, no messages. Nothing at all. The phone felt new yet old at the same time.

It was like it had been wiped clean.

But that wasn't his headache. Unbothered, Brian downloaded some games to pass the time and wasted the evening with the phone in hand.

Playing and laughing.

That night, however, something strange happened.

While Brian lay asleep, the phone on his nightstand began to glow. A faint, eerie blue light flickered from its screen, but Brian, deep in his dreams, didn't notice. And soon the screen went dark.

The next day, Max didn't show up to school. Brian overheard some kids saying that Max had stayed home after being scolded for losing the phone.

However, Brian didn't care.

When he got home, he ran to his room and tossed his bag on the bed. The mobile was where Brian had left it the previous night and he reached for it to continue his game.

Surprisingly, the phone was locked. He didn't set any password. Confused, he tried again, but nothing worked.

Then the phone glowed and a message appeared on the lock screen:

'You've been a bad kid, Brian. Time to pay for your sins.'

"YOU'VE BEEN A BAD KID, BRIAN.
TIME TO PAY FOR YOUR SINS."

Brian blinked. What kind of joke was this? He tried to turn the phone off, but, as if the device had a life of its own, it wasn't turning off. Then another message popped up:

'You need to do exactly what I say or there will be consequences.'

Brian chuckled nervously. What could a phone do?

It was a bluff, he thought, but then a scream came from the hall. It was his sister.

Brian rushed to her door, but it was locked, even though the latch was on the inside. No matter how hard he pulled, it wouldn't budge. His sister was shouting, pounding on the door, terrified.

Panicked, Brian screamed in the air, "Fine! I'll do everything you say."

Instantly, the door clicked open. His sister rushed out, scared but unharmed. Brian tried to calm his sister down, knowing she had no idea what had happened. However, Brian did and he was pale as a ghost.

The phone must be possessed, he muttered and tried to smash it once he was back in his room, but then another warning showed on the screen:

'You can't escape me.'

The kid knew better than to ignore the message. He realized that the phone was telling the truth. It would really haunt him until he did what was asked.

He was trapped. The phone gave him his first task – *Make paper planes and throw them during class when the teacher is looking.*

Brian was horrified. If he did that he would surely get into trouble, so gritting his teeth in anger, he yelled, "No! I won't."

The room fell quiet. And then... *ding...* a message appeared.

'Look inside your closet.'

Brian didn't want to, but something pulled him to open the door. Inside, his favorite PS5 was smashed in half. He gasped.

'Do what I say or I'll keep destroying.'

It warned.

The phone even set a countdown timer, showing that he only had until the next day to complete his task.

The following day, Brian hesitated to get out of bed and go to school. But what choice did he have? The phone was more sinister than he was.

At school, when the teacher was taking attendance, with his hands shaking, Brian stood up. He closed his eyes and breathed out before throwing paper planes everywhere.

The teacher was furious. For the first time, Brian was scolded and although he got a lighter punishment, which was to stand during the whole first period, he felt humiliated.

Kids whispered and pointed, just as he had always done to others.

However, it was just the beginning.

Brian believed the phone had gone mad when in the evening he read the next task - *Chew gum, make a big ball out of them, and stick it in your hair.*

Brian cursed his luck. The phone was making him do what he had done to others.

Brian groaned in frustration. He liked his appearance, and the thought of gum in his hair made him cringe.

So, he plainly refused. But as soon as he did so, he heard a loud *pop*. His favorite signed football had just burst.

Defeated and scared, Brian chewed some gum and reluctantly mashed it into his hair. His parents were shocked when they saw him and his mother had to shave his head, warning him to be more careful next time.

If only they knew.

When he went to school the next day, Brian could feel all eyes on him. The kids wanted to laugh at his bald head but they realized that Brian was this close to losing it. Hence, they avoided him.

But the phone wasn't done with him *yet*.

The tasks got weirder and worse. The next day, the phone demanded that Brian skip lunch and serve food to the kids he had bullied. With his stomach growling, Brian served food in the cafeteria, watching as others got full plates while he went hungry.

The kid who he bullied for eating lunch looked at him with hatred but Brian was too ashamed to lift his head.

Finally, the last task came. The phone ordered Brian to return it to Max and confess in front of the whole class that he had stolen it.

This one was going to hurt his pride.

Brian's stomach churned. Apologizing? In front of everyone?

That night Brian couldn't sleep. He dreaded what was to come, but the thought of finally being free from the device was tempting.

The next day, Max was surprised when Brian handed him his phone. By then the phone was unlocked.

"I... I stole your phone, Max," Brian said, his voice cracking. Max blinked, clearly surprised but eventually accepted the apology. The kid was grateful that at least his grandpa's gift didn't fall into some stranger's hand.

Brian realized his mistake. He was truly ashamed of himself and turning around, he apologized to every kid he had made fun of or bullied into submission.

There was a stunned silence. Some kids stared at him in disbelief while others whispered.

Some accepted his apology while others, too hurt to forgive, turned away.

Brian felt like a weight had lifted from his shoulders. That night, back at home, everything that had been destroyed—his PS5, his football—was suddenly back to normal, as if nothing had ever happened.

From then onwards Brian became kinder and more helpful. Whenever he saw bullies tormenting others, he stood up to them.

Because Brian knew that no prank or no joke was worth the terrifying experience he'd gone through.

Chapter 13

The Cabin in the Woods

On a bright summer afternoon, Theo, John, Mia, and Emma were bubbling with excitement. They had finally made it to the woods for their weekend getaway!

The cabin belonged to Theo's Uncle Steve who had told them that it was the perfect place for an adventure. "You kids are going to love it," he had said.

A week away from their boring college life – what could go wrong?

The group arrived at the trailhead, where they noticed two paths going in opposite directions. Both had arrows. The left path had the address Uncle Steve gave them, number 21, while the right had the number 22 painted on it.

"Uncle Steve said to take the left path. His cabin number is 21," Theo said confidently, and off they went.

After a short walk, they finally reached the cabin. It looked... old. The wood creaked and the roof was leaking. But it had charm.

Surrounded by tall trees and the sweet scent of pine, the place seemed peaceful. They didn't mind its shabby look. After all, it was theirs for the whole weekend.

"This is awesome!" John said, dropping his bag. "We've got the whole place to ourselves!"

"Sure," Mia replied, eyeing the cabin with a smirk. "If you ignore the fact that it looks like it belongs in a ghost story."

Emma shivered. "Don't start with that stuff."

They unpacked, ate a quick dinner, and decided to call it an early night, too tired to chat.

The next morning, they were up and out early, ready to hike up the nearby hill. The sun shone brightly as they followed the trail, chatting and stopping to take in the beauty of the forest.

At the top, John scanned the horizon. "Where's the cabin?"

The group looked down at the sea of trees below, but the cabin was nowhere in sight.

"Weird," Mia said, furrowing her brow. "It should be right there."

Theo shrugged. "These woods are huge. Maybe we are looking in the wrong direction," he said.

No one was too concerned, so they shrugged it off and headed back down. The rest of the day passed quickly, filled with games and exploring the forest around the cabin.

That night, however, things got strange.

John woke up in the middle of the night, needing to use the bathroom. He crawled out of his sleeping bag, but as he tiptoed to the door, he froze.

There was a sound coming from above. It was faint at first—a creaking noise, like someone... or something... walking on the roof.

His heart skipped a beat. He listened, hoping it was just the wind. But the creaking continued.

"Theo, wake up," John whispered, shaking his friend. "There's someone on the roof."

Theo rubbed his eyes, groaning, but the moment he heard the noise, he shot up. They woke the others, and soon all four of them listened quietly as the creaks continued.

"Let's check it out," Theo suggested, grabbing a flashlight.

They tiptoed outside, shining the beam across the roof. The creaking stopped. And then they saw that the roof was empty.

"Maybe it was an animal," John said, though his voice wasn't as confident as usual.

"Probably just some raccoon or something," Mia added.

Still uneasy, they convinced themselves it was nothing to worry about. Perhaps they had all imagined the sound. But John was still scared. He asked Theo to accompany him to the bathroom, which was a little away from the cabin.

The night air was chilly, and as Theo stood outside guarding the place, he suddenly felt a presence—like someone was behind him.

He turned quickly, his heart racing, but saw nothing but trees. However, Theo was a little creeped out. He and John hurried back to the cabin and the rest of the night passed without any weird incident.

Days passed, and the strange incidents faded from their minds. The group kept busy exploring the woods, playing games, and enjoying the freedom of being away from everything.

But then on their last night, something else happened.

Theo woke up first. This time, it wasn't a creak or rustle that caught his attention. It was movement outside the window. He squinted, rubbing his eyes, and there, standing in the shadows of the trees, was a man.

His heart raced, but as his eyes adjusted, he recognized the figure. "Uncle Steve?" he whispered to himself.

Excited, he went outside. Sure enough, Uncle Steve stood with a warm smile. "Surprise!" he yelled.

Theo woke the others. "Guys, Uncle Steve's here!"

"Uncle Steve!" Emma cheered. "We didn't think you'd come!"

"Well, I couldn't let you have all the fun without me, could I?" Uncle Steve replied and chuckled.

They went inside the cabin and that night, they stayed up late, laughing and telling stories around the fire. It felt like the perfect way to end their trip.

The next morning, Uncle Steve mentioned he had to stick around to do some repairs around the cabin. He told the kids they should head out first and that he'd catch up with them later.

So, they packed up their things and started down the trail, laughing and talking about the fun weekend they had. But as they reached the trailhead—the spot where the two paths divided—Theo's phone buzzed. It was Uncle Steve.

"How was the cabin?" Uncle Steve asked.

Theo blinked, confused. "Uh... it was great! But you already know that. You were there."

There was a long pause on the other end of the line. "What are you talking about?" Uncle Steve sounded confused. "I've been at home all weekend."

Theo's heart skipped a beat. He argued with his uncle, stating that they all stayed in cabin number 21, which was on the left side of the trail.

"No, Theo," Uncle Steve's voice was firm. "Wait, what did you say?" His voice was shaky. Then after a long pause, Uncle Steve spoke, "Theo, my cabin is number 21 but it is on the right path of the trail."

Theo froze. He slowly turned to look back at the signpost. The arrows had been swapped. The number 21, which had pointed to the left when they arrived, now pointed to the right.

His voice shook as he replied. "I... I think we stayed at the wrong cabin."

There was another pause. "Theo, there *is* no other cabin out there. Get out of those woods. Now!" Uncle Steve warned and without a second thought, they ran as fast as they could down the path.

They sprinted down the trail, hearts pounding, not daring to look back. When they finally reached the road, they collapsed, breathless and terrified.

After that day, they never spoke of the cabin again. No one ever figured out where they had stayed... or who the man claiming to be Uncle Steve really was.

But one thing was for sure—they wouldn't be visiting that part of the woods again anytime soon.

We Hope You Enjoyed the Journey!

Thank you for joining us on this spooky adventure! If these tales kept you entertained, we'd be thrilled if you could take a moment to share your thoughts by leaving a quick review on Amazon. Your feedback not only helps other readers discover this book but also supports us in creating more exciting stories!

Simply visit: www.amazon.com/review/create-review?&asin=B0D HSTPGTR

Or scan the QR code below to go directly to the review page!

Thank you for your support, and we hope to see you again on the next adventure!

Made in the USA
Monee, IL
27 October 2024

68642097R00056